...THE...
RAINBOW
SOLUTION

Written by Sue Cason
Illustrated by Peter Foster
Designed by Peter Shaw

Published by Mimosa Publications Pty Ltd
PO Box 779, Hawthorn 3122, Australia
© 1995 Mimosa Publications Pty Ltd
All rights reserved

Literacy 2000 is a Trademark registered in the
United States Patent and Trademark Office.

Distributed in the United States of America by

Rigby
A Division of Reed Elsevier Inc.
500 Coventry Lane
Crystal Lake, IL 60014
800-822-8661

Distributed in Canada by
PRENTICE HALL GINN
1870 Birchmount Road
Scarborough
Ontario M1P 2J7

99 98 97 96
10 9 8 7 6 5 4 3 2
Printed in Hong Kong through Bookbuilders Ltd

ISBN 0 7327 1579 2

...THE...
RAINBOW
SOLUTION

Sue Cason
Illustrated by Peter Foster

I COULDN'T BELIEVE MY EYES! But there it was, huge and sleek, padding across the kitchen floor toward me. As it drew close it growled deep in its throat, and then rubbed its face around my legs.

Mom and Dad were standing back, their faces beaming, waiting for me to say something. Grandpa was with them, too, and even he was smiling.

"For me?" I managed to gasp. "Mom, Dad … this is … this … this is the pet of my dreams! You shouldn't have!"

"You deserve it, Riley darling," said Mom.

"And we knew you had your heart set on this rare South American jaguar," said Dad.

5

"Yes, indeed," said Grandpa, stroking the jaguar's head. "A special pet for a special boy. And if you ever need someone to look after it or take it for walks while you're at school, then just you let me know."

I couldn't think what to say, except, "Gosh, thanks! Thanks, everyone."

The jaguar started nuzzling me again, growling its deep jaguar-purr of contentment. Then it jumped up and planted its front paws on my chest with an affectionate, heavy thud.

And another thud, and … suddenly I opened my eyes. Where was the sleek beast of the jungle? All I could see was Mom leaning over me with my baby brother, Max, wriggling in her arms. He was grinning a toothy grin and banging me on the chest.

"Aaaahh! What are you doing?" I yelped.

"Waking you up, of course," said Mom, "or else you'll be late for school."

JUST MY LUCK: ALL A DREAM! I thought it was too good to be true – especially the part about a happy Grandpa. Back in the real world, Grandpa (who, along with Grandma, lived next door to us) didn't seem to be happy about very much at all. Grumbling seemed to be the only thing that kept him busy, and he'd made his feelings about pets very clear!

"They're a liability!" he said. "Always clawing walls, digging gardens, making a noise, and annoying the neighbors. Nothing but a nuisance!"

Mom and Dad had said that I could get a pet. But if I did we'd probably have to listen to complaints like that every day.

No, thanks! For the moment I'd just consider my options. Hopefully Grandpa was only going through a "stage" and would cheer up soon. And in the meantime, at least I had Boris, Boris the goldfish. There he was, waving his filmy fins gracefully as I walked past his bowl on the way to get some breakfast.

Roxanne, my sister, was heading for the kitchen, too. "Don't forget to take Boris for his morning walk. Or if he isn't up to it, maybe you should think about getting a Mexican walking fish. Or a piranha or two – they'd be fun to play with. But you'd have to get a bowl with a fence around it."

Roxanne was always coming up with helpful pet suggestions like that. Typical sister – she just didn't seem to take me seriously!

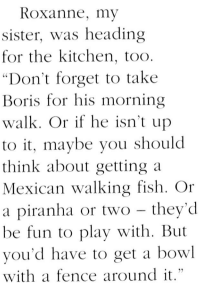

9

WHEN I WALKED INTO THE KITCHEN, I saw a mysterious carton on the kitchen table. It was mysterious because someone had written "EAT ME!" across the top. I turned the box around and read what was printed on the side: "New! Apricot and sesame seed health bars. High in fiber, high in energy, high in taste ..."

"Hi in there," yawned a sleepy voice from the hallway. "Found my surprise?"

It was Dad, in his crumpled striped pajamas. I hadn't expected to see him. "I didn't hear you come home, Dad," I said.

He tousled my hair. "I sneaked in when you were asleep."

This made me feel like laughing out loud. My father doesn't sneak – he lumbers like a great big bear!

"Yep," said Dad, "I just eased Herc down the side of the house and crept inside. No one could've heard me."

Herc is Dad's truck: a huge twenty-two-wheeled semitrailer painted all the colors of the rainbow and more. HERCULES is written in big bold letters across the front, and on the back it says,

RAINBOW TRANSPORT * WE GO
ANYWHERE * BILL RAINBOW.
Dad drives Hercules all over the
country, delivering goods to
supermarkets and all kinds of stores.

Over breakfast I told Mom and Dad about my dream. "You gave me a pet jaguar," I said, pouring some cereal into a bowl. "It was great! Even Grandpa liked it."

Dad laughed. "Keep dreaming!" he said.

"But you know you can get another pet," Mom said, "if you're sure you want one, and if you can decide what sort of pet you want. Preferably not a jaguar!"

"Try something more common – like an elephant or a mongoose!" put in Roxanne.

"Ha-ha, very funny." I gave her what I hoped was a withering look. "I just don't want to rush into it," I said. "And I think that anything noisier than Boris might cause a lot of trouble with our next-door neighbors."

As if what I'd said had set off some kind of explosion, there was a sudden pounding at the back door. In burst Grandpa like a jack-in-the-box, shaking his fist. "What do you mean, coming home in the middle of the night and making all that noise! You woke everybody up!" He glared at Dad.

"I thought I came in fairly quietly,
Cyrus," said Dad, scratching his head.

Grandpa's eyes glinted like two small
emeralds. "Quietly? Quietly? You don't
know what the word means!"

15

For a moment, I thought Grandpa was going to send Dad to his room, or tell him that he was grounded. It didn't seem fair. "Dad can't make the truck any quieter," I said.

Grandpa ignored me completely.

"I'm sorry," said Dad, "but when I do the run to River City, I can't get home any earlier. If it's any consolation, I don't do that run again for two weeks."

"It's no consolation," snapped Grandpa, "no consolation whatsoever!"

"Cyrus," said Mom firmly, "there's nothing we can do about it. Bill can't change his job, and you've never complained about Herc before. Please try to be reasonable."

"Reasonable?" Grandpa shouted. "I'll show you reasonable!"

"Now look," soothed Dad, "what say you go home and calm down. I'll see what I can do in future about coming in even more quietly, okay?" He steered Grandpa out the back door, closed the door, and leaned against it with a dramatic sigh.

"Welcome home, Dad," I said.

Grandma popped her head around
the door. "Has Cyrus been in here
annoying you again?"

Dad nodded and grinned.

"I don't think he has enough to do,"
she said. "He drives me crazy. If anyone
has any bright ideas about helping him
keep busy, let me know. That might
keep us all happy!"

"Yes," said Mom, "but right now *I've*
got to get busy. I'd better go to work or
I'll be late."

"Okay," said Dad, "I'll take Max to his daycare, then wash the dust off Herc. After that I'm off to Black Mountain. I'll be back in the middle of the afternoon tomorrow, so I'll avoid waking the touchy part of the neighborhood. Then I have almost three whole days at home."

I asked Dad what he was taking to Black Mountain.

"Now let me see," he said thoughtfully. "I think it's a truckload of money, and naturally they'll give me some free samples."

"In your dreams, Dad," grinned my cheeky sister. "In your dreams."

Oh well, at least Dad didn't seem to be letting Grandpa get him down. Rainbow by name and rainbow by nature – that was my dad.

IT LOOKED AS THOUGH GRANDPA had found himself something to do. As we left for school we saw him out in the yard, sanding paint from his front gate. Nearby, on the path, was a large can of paint with a paintbrush resting on its lid.

"That'll keep you busy, Grandpa!" Roxanne called as she closed our gate. He grunted and kept sanding.

"Yes," I thought to myself, "and a busy Grandpa is a happy Grandpa – we hope."

THAT AFTERNOON, I WAS HELPING MOM look for weeds in the garden while Max played happily on the grass. Roxanne was at a friend's place. It seemed like a good time to discuss some new ideas I'd had about quiet, trouble-free pets.

"Mom," I began, "I passed the pet store on the way home and they've got two guinea pigs for sale. What do you think?"

"I think they'd be cheaper to feed than a jaguar!" laughed Mom. "What do *you* think?"

"I think they're cute, and they'd keep each other company, and they're very quiet. I can't see how anyone could object." (Meaning Grandpa, of course!)

"Maybe," said Mom, "but there are other things to consider."

"Such as?"

"Breeding! Guinea pigs, mice, and rabbits! They all tend to get out of control."

"Oliver's mice haven't," I said, thinking of the two twitchy-nosed mice in my friend's bedroom. "Oliver's mice are totally in control."

"And how long has he had them?"
asked Mom, pulling out a thistle.
"Since Friday."

"Hmmm," she said, "let's see how many he has next month. Why don't you find out at the pet store if ..."

Suddenly a door banged next door. Out came Grandpa, furiously waving a paintbrush. "When is that good-for-nothing son of mine due back?" he yelled. "He's ruined my front gate!"

"Ruined your front gate, Cyrus?" Mom said. "How on earth ...?"

"Ruined! Ruined! I painted it this morning and now it's spotted and streaked and spoiled. Someone's splashed water all over it deliberately, and I bet I know who. That son of mine, washing that truck of his!"

Mom frowned. "I'm afraid I really don't know anything about it. But if anything like that did happen, I know

that it would have been an accident.
I'll talk to Bill as soon as he gets home
tomorrow."

"Don't bother!" snapped Grandpa. "I'll
repaint the thing myself, right now, so
the paint dries while he's not in the
same State."

I heard Mom mutter something under
her breath, and I decided to leave the
subject of pets till another day.

When I got home the next day, I told Dad what had happened. But he already knew – and he'd already said he was sorry. Now he was sitting in our kitchen with Grandma, and they both looked amazingly relaxed and happy.

"Your Grandma and I have had an idea," Dad told me. "We were thinking how badly this whole house needs a fresh coat of paint. And we think that Grandpa might really enjoy helping. As soon as your mom gets home we're going to talk to her about it."

Mom thought it was a great idea. "You're right about the place needing painting," she said. "The paint's even peeling off in places. Only the spiderwebs are holding it on. And if Grandpa wants to help, he'd be very welcome."

"It's just what he needs!" sighed Grandma. "And he adores painting. You know he's painted every part of our house twice in the last three years. I wouldn't let him do it this year – I told him the rooms were getting smaller because of all those layers of paint! I'll go and tell him right now." She flung her arms around Dad and hugged him. "I think you might have saved my sanity."

Everyone seemed very confident that the painting was a good idea. I only hoped they were right.

MY BEDROOM WALLS SHUDDERED as though a storm had hit. I leaped out of bed, nearly bumping into Dad who was striding past my door in his pajamas.

"What on earth …?"

Roxanne stood frowning and rubbing her eyes. Mom hauled a bewildered, wailing Max out of his crib, and we all trailed after Dad.

Dust swirled in through the open
kitchen window. Dad threw open the
back door. There was Grandpa, wearing
a face mask and ancient goggles,
standing on a stepladder near the back
wall of the house. He steered a whining
sander along the wooden boards. My
heart sank. Trouble and Grandpa
seemed to go together.

He suddenly noticed his audience
and turned off the sander. "Morning!" he
called, as the motor droned to a stop.
"Thought I'd make an early start. Didn't
think you'd mind."

"Mind?" said Mom. "Mind? Why didn't you give us some warning?"

"Warning?" said Grandpa. "What warning?"

"Grandpa," said Roxanne, "it's six-thirty in the morning. That's very early to begin a demolition job on the house."

"Especially while we're still inside," I said, as I wiped Max's tear-stained face.

"Well," said Grandpa in a surprised voice, "I thought you'd be grateful. You were the ones who wanted the house painted, weren't you?"

Roxanne shook her head, turned, and stomped back inside. I knew just how she felt.

"How long do you think this sanding will take?" asked Mom.

"No more than a day or two," answered Grandpa. "Shouldn't be a problem, should it?"

"Not for anyone who goes out for the day," said Dad.

Grandpa snorted, and adjusted his goggles. The sander roared into action, attacking the wall.

THE DUST SETTLED ON EVERYTHING and everybody. And it was still only eight o'clock.

"Thank goodness for school!" I yelled to Roxanne, grabbing my bag.

"Let's go early today!" she yelled back.

"Thank goodness for work!" shouted Mom. "Come on, Maxie, even your daycare is more peaceful than this." She hoisted him from his high chair.

"Have a good day," Dad sighed, and he waved forlornly as we all trooped out the back door.

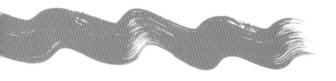

IT WAS LATE AFTERNOON. We were all sitting in Grandma's loungeroom, watching Dad and Grandpa working together. It was amazing. They'd almost finished – and they weren't fighting.

"Well, so far, so good," I said.

Grandma sat with Max on her knee. They were both looking at a picture book. "Sally, I am really happy that you

and Bill are letting Cyrus do this," she said to Mom.

Mom smiled. "That's quite okay. It would have taken us ages. It's silly to look a gift horse in the mouth."

Max pointed to a picture of a horse in his book. "'Orse!" he announced.

Mom put down her coffee cup and came over. "Have you had any more ideas about a pet?"

"I was thinking about ... a goat," I replied.

Roxanne put down her homework. "A goat? You've got to be joking! Not nearly exotic enough. What you need is a jumping kangaroo!"

"Thanks a lot, Roxanne," I said. "I think a goat would be great. It could eat the grass and I wouldn't have to mow the lawn. Oliver's cousin has a

goat. It does tricks and follows him everywhere. It's not very noisy, either."

"Goats can eat more than grass, dear," said Grandma. "When I was a child we had a goat, and it always wanted to eat the wash."

She was probably right. And anyway, I still wasn't in a hurry to make up my mind. First I wanted to see if the entire Rainbow household was going to survive the painting.

MAYBE THE CHORUS OF BIRDS WOKE ME next morning, but more likely it was the strong smell of … What was it? I got out of bed and opened the curtains to throw some light on the subject.

Of course! There was Grandpa, right outside my bedroom, slapping pink undercoat on the wall. He waved cheerfully and kept on painting. Amazing! Grandpa was in a good mood for the second day in a row!

"Phew, what a smell," I said, and Grandpa actually grinned. Then I caught sight of Dad, painting the wall from the other end. Dad saw me, too, and waved his brush. He looked just as happy as Grandpa.

Then Roxanne called from outside my door: "Riley, I've got the ideal pet for you … a carnivorous plant.

Low maintenance, very cheap and very entertaining!"

Great – another of Roxanne's jokes. "Oh – ha ha ha!" I said sarcastically.

"And do you want a mail-order coupon for crocodile eggs?" she asked.

HANDLE WITH CARE

WHEN WE CAME HOME FROM SCHOOL, we were greeted by a house entirely covered in undercoat pink. Dad was washing brushes. Mom and Grandma were admiring the paintwork.

"Well, Bill," Grandpa said, "I think we've done a pretty good job."

"Yes," Dad agreed. "But unfortunately I'll only be able to paint in the morning tomorrow. I've got a run to Cape Baskerville in the afternoon. But I'll be back on Saturday."

"Hmm," said Grandpa, "I'd come for the ride, but I'm keen to keep painting."

"Maybe next time," Dad replied.

Roxanne and I stood with our mouths open at this display of affection.

"We're still discussing the color scheme," said Dad. "We'll put an order in at the hardware store tomorrow."

"There's only one color this house should be, and that's white. White all over," declared Grandpa.

"All white?"

"Yep," said Grandpa, "it would save time and be cheaper, too. I happen to know that Antarctic White is on special this week."

Dad scratched his chin. "I think we'd like a bit of color on the house, Cyrus. You know – all white is a bit stark. We'll think about it, and we'll let you know in the morning."

THE WHOLE FAMILY SAT AROUND the kitchen table studying color charts: Dad, Mom, Roxanne, and me. Max was asleep.

"They're such beautiful colors," said Dad admiringly. "It's a pity we can't use every single one."

The colors *were* beautiful, I thought. Midnight Blue. Hibiscus Scarlet. Juicy Orange. Colorado Red. Pine Tree Green. Parrot Pink. Summer Sea Turquoise. Pineapple Crush Yellow. Twilight Purple. Pigeon Gray. Golden Sunlight. Clotted Cream …

"Summer Sea Turquoise would go nicely with Pineapple Crush Yellow," Mom suggested.

"I like the idea of Colorado Red doors and Clotted Cream on the windows and gutters," said Roxanne.

"How about Twilight Purple and Juicy Orange together?" I ventured.

"Hmmm," mumbled Dad, "this could be more difficult than I thought. Personally, I like Pigeon Gray with Parrot Pink and Midnight Blue."

Each of us began arguing the merits of our own color schemes.

"Stop!" said Mom. "We're obviously in agreement on one thing – bright, not white! But this is getting us nowhere. Dad and I will narrow it down to one or two, and we can make our final choice tomorrow morning."

"Couldn't we do something a bit easier?" asked Dad. "Like climb Mt. Everest before bedtime?"

BREAKFAST TIME. There was a scuffling sound outside the kitchen. I opened the back door and there was Grandpa, already in his overalls and carrying a can of paint. "Good morning," he said cheerfully, "I'm ready for work."

"I'm sorry, Cyrus, we still haven't made up our minds about the colors for the trimmings," Dad said.

"No problem," said Grandpa. "I ordered enough Antarctic White to paint the whole house. And it's arrived already, special early delivery." He waggled the paintbrush and began to climb the ladder.

"Well," said Dad, "all right. But only paint the walls. We'll do the trimmings later in the week."

Grandpa saluted with his brush. "Aye, aye, Captain."

Mom closed the door. "I don't suppose he can do any harm. We'll talk more about the colors when you get back from Cape Baskerville."

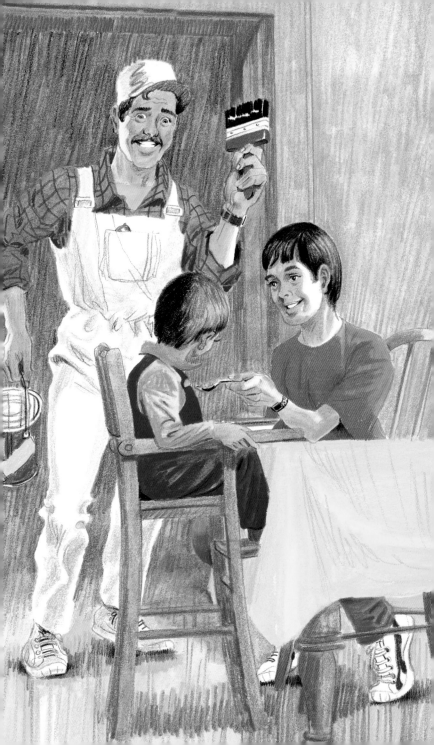

BY FRIDAY AFTERNOON we had a white house – an all-white house – and Grandpa was obviously feeling triumphant. "Finished!" he cried, as Roxanne and I came up the drive. "Look how clean and fresh and white it is. Antarctic White! Magnificent!"

We didn't need to look. We'd seen the house gleaming at us all the way from the corner. It looked clean and

white and fresh all right, just like an enormous iceberg that had lost its way!

Grandma came from next door and joined us. Mom came home from work with Maxie. Together we all stood and stared.

"Beautiful, isn't it?" said Grandpa innocently.

"Wait till Bill gets home and sees it," said Grandma grimly.

It wasn't only Dad, I thought; none of us had expected this. Rainbow by name; rainbow by nature. Riley Rainbow, Roxanne Rainbow, Bill and Sally Rainbow, Maxie Rainbow …

And suddenly the solution was in front of me. I was going to make sure that we brightened up Grandpa's great white iceberg before Dad got home. And I knew what colors I needed.

I could hardly wait to tell Roxanne, but I wanted it to be a surprise for Mom and Dad. Luckily, Mom had a seminar to attend the next day. I was nearly bursting with my secret by the time her car pulled out of the drive.

"Guess what! The answer was in front of us all the time."

Roxanne frowned. "It was? What answer? I don't even remember the question."

"Listen. We're going to paint the trimmings. And I know what colors to choose. Rainbow colors! We're all Rainbows! Do you get it?"

She smiled. "I get it, Riley Rainbow. But what are we going to do about it?"

I put Max into his playpen on the lawn. "Find the color charts for a start," I said.

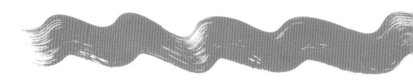

WE WERE BENT OVER the color charts when Grandma came around the corner of the house. We'd already chosen three colors: Hibiscus Scarlet, Juicy Orange, and Pineapple Crush.

"Oh, there you are. I've just dropped in to see how you're getting on. Grandpa's gone off shopping ..." She must have noticed the guilty looks on our faces. "Now, what are you two up to?" she said.

Roxanne and I looked at each other and decided to tell her.

"So you've already chosen the red, orange, and yellow," she said with a grin. "Now, what about …?"

"Easy," I said, flipping open the color chart. "Pine Tree Green, Summer Sea Turquoise …"

"Midnight Blue, and Twilight Purple," finished Roxanne.

"Beautiful!" said Grandma. She dialed the phone number of the hardware store. "This is Mrs. Nellie Rainbow speaking. I want to order some more paint. Could you deliver it immediately? Here are the colors: Pine Tree Green …"

ROXANNE HAD PAINTED the back door a striking Summer Sea Turquoise. Now she was painting the front door Juicy Orange and Hibiscus Scarlet. Grandma slapped paint on the last of the Midnight Blue window frames at the back of the house. They made a nice contrast to the Pineapple Crush Yellow frames and Hibiscus Scarlet shutters at the front.

I was up on the ladder painting the guttering a glowing Twilight Purple and telling Roxanne to work faster.

"Don't rush me," she retorted.

"Please don't argue," said Grandma. "There's no time. They could all be home at any minute."

We painted in silence for a while, until an unmistakable sound broke into the peaceful afternoon.

"I can hear Herc! Paint faster!"

"Slow down," said Roxanne. "We don't want to spoil the paint job at the last minute!"

It was then I saw Herc's bright red cab appear above the tops of the houses. Herc rounded the corner and Dad eased the huge vehicle into the driveway.

At the same moment, Mom's car pulled up at the front of the house. Grandpa was walking along the pavement. Dad, his mouth open in wonder, turned off Herc's motor and got out of the cab. Mom went and stood beside him. Grandpa sleepwalked into the drive, gaping like Boris the goldfish on a bad day.

I climbed down the ladder. "Well, do you like it?" I could see they were taking it all in, soaking up the brilliance of the colors. Hibiscus Scarlet, Juicy Orange, Pineapple Crush Yellow, Summer Sea Turquoise, Midnight Blue, Twilight Purple. All the colors of the rainbow.

We watched as they stared at the gutterings, the window frames, the doors …

"Riley," breathed Mom. "Roxanne …"

"What …!" Grandpa's voice was the only unhappy one.

"Rainbow by name, rainbow by habitat," gasped Dad. "Fantastic!"

"Hmm," murmured Grandpa, looking around at all our happy faces. "The Antarctic White picks up those colors quite well, don't you think?"

"Do you really like it?" I asked. "I mean, do you *really* like it?"

"It's beautiful," said Mom and Dad.

Roxanne sighed happily. "We haven't started the eaves yet."

"Let me guess," grinned Dad. "Pine Tree …"

"… Green," I said with a smile.

"Great!" said Dad. "But all the painting can wait for a minute. I have a surprise of my own to show you. Wait till you see the free sample on Herc's front seat."

"Not more health food bars, I hope," said Roxanne. "We have enough to last for months!"

"Have a look for yourselves," said Dad.

I opened Herc's door and there it was, a small carton containing … a puppy.

"Dad!" I shouted. "A dog!"

"They had a litter at the Baskerville roadhouse, and there was just this one pup that they hadn't found a home for yet. I couldn't resist!"

I lifted the puppy from the carton. She was plump and black and white, and her fur was as soft as silk.

"I hope you'll be very happy together," said Dad, laughing.

Roxanne stroked the pup's head. "Now," she said, "this is what I call a

real pet. Thanks, Dad, you've saved us from goats and carnivorous plants!"

The puppy snuggled into my arms. "This is the best week," I said. "The very best week."

AS WE STOOD ADMIRING THE PUPPY and the rainbow-colored house, Grandpa leaned across to Grandma. "Now tell me, Nellie, how do you feel about a bit of color to brighten up our place? I'm beginning to think it looks a bit stark as it is."

Grandma smiled and took him by the arm. "Let's talk about it at home," she said, "and leave the others in peace for awhile."

Grandpa patted the pup again before he headed off. "Lovely pup you have there, young Riley," he smiled. "And if you ever need someone to help look after it or take it for walks when you're at school, then just you let me know."

TITLES IN THE SERIES

SET 9A

Television Drama
Time for Sale
The Shady Deal
The Loch Ness Monster Mystery
Secrets of the Desert

SET 9B

To JJ From CC
Pandora's Box
The Birthday Disaster
The Song of the Mantis
Helping the Hoiho

SET 9C

Glumly
Rupert and the Griffin
The Tree, the Trunk, and the Tuba
Errol the Peril
Cassidy's Magic

SET 9D

Barney
Get a Grip, Pip!
Casey's Case
Dear Future
Strange Meetings

SET 10A

A Battle of Words
The Rainbow Solution
Fortune's Friend
Eureka
It's a Frog's Life

SET 10B

The Cat Burglar of Pethaven Drive
The Matchbox
In Search of the Great Bears
Many Happy Returns
Spider Relatives

SET 10C

Horrible Hank
Brian's Brilliant Career
Fernitickles
It's All in Your Mind,
    James Robert
Wing High, Gooftah

SET 10D

The Week of the Jellyhoppers
Timothy Whuffenpuffen-
    Whippersnapper
Timedetectors
Ryan's Dog Ringo
The Secret of Kiribu Tapu Lagoon